GUARDIANS

GUARDIANS

AN ABOMINATION IS BORN

JONATHAN MOTEN

iUniverse, Inc.
Bloomington

Guardians
An Abomination is born

iUniverse books may be ordered through booksellers or by contacting:

iUniverse
1663 Liberty Drive
Bloomington, IN 47403
www.iuniverse.com
1-800-Authors (1-800-288-4677)

ISBN: 978-1-4620-0333-4 (sc)
ISBN: 978-1-4620-0334-1 (e)

Printed in the United States of America

iUniverse rev. date: 10/17/2011

TABLE OF CONTENTS

Dedication to Yin and Yang

The dedication of this book is

Split and **Mixed** in **two** ways.

It is dedicated to **Yin** and **Yang**

, **Good** and **Evil.**

It is dedicated to the ones, who said,

My book **would make it**,

And the ones that said

It wouldn't, for if it wasn't, **for you both**

I wouldn't be where I am.

Prologue

THE DEATH WISH

My name is Destiny. Yes, the being that determines who you fall in love with. The one that says, "You are meant to do this." And for the many millennia I have done so. Thanking of humans, witches, demons, death, and that of decay. I am the one who says you will die in the next two seconds, and oh, how jealous I am of those I speak those words to.

As I have said, I have done so over many millennia, millennia mind you, but now I find that I, like many others in my position of immortality, are weary of the multiple years, decades, centuries, and so on, moving past as if they do not notice me. My life expectancy is a ridiculous one, and it must come to a halt. Though it is near impossible to kill a perpetual being, and is why I haven't performed the act myself. There is only one power to kill an ever-lasting creature. It is that of the Council, a group of Beings of the Light and Demons of the Abyss that hold control of the magical world.

I began to come up with the plan for my execution. See, there are laws created by the Council to keep everything in order. The highest law is that good and evil can not mix. If this law was broken then those of cause where to be killed. Therefore I went to work.

I traveled to Greece, to the great Mountain of Olympus, to find Aphrodite. I told her of my plan. She new the risk and what I asked of her. Then with that she was happy to oblige. I asked her to use her power on a High Witch of a covenant, Mara Hew, and a Demon General, Verex.

Aphrodite walked out onto a balcony. The floor of the balcony was crystal clear water. Beautiful sea shells where laid down as stepping stones. The bottom of her pink silk dress gently moved over the water. The top and middle blew gently in the wind. The sun shined bright, like early morning on the right of her. Here golden hair shined brighter than that of the sun. Aphrodite's blue eyes sparkled like diamonds. She raised her hands up level to her shoulders. Her skin looked so delicate that it looks like if you had touched her, she would have shattered to glass.

Her hands began to glow a bright pink. Two energy balls formed in her hands. She bent her elbows back, and then shot her hands forward. The energy balls took off like snakes in the clouds. They dove down, out of the clouds, and to the hard rock and stone that was earth. One of them pulled up and flew but a few feet over land, but the other went into the deep earth. The one that was flying over earth now flew over the ocean to America. The other one tore through the underworld into the land of Hades. It went into a portal, which leads to another world, and a place of demons.

In the state of Virginia, a woman was in her house cleaning dishes. She had long brown hair, and tan skin. She was about five-five and had brown eyes. Her hair was messy, and she had house clothes on. She only had her son in the house. As she washed the dishes, she thought about stuff like, was she hungry? If she was, what would she eat? The occasional, "I could use a man." thought came to mind a few times. After she set all the dishes on the towel to dry, she took the rag and wiped down the counters. Then the pink light ran through the door, and ran into her back. Her eyes lit up bright. Only people who have experienced true love would know what Mara was felling, but only if they multiplied it times a thousand.

Mara fell to the ground. Her mind was taken away to a beautiful and pure land. She was standing in a field of tall grass. Birds singing above her, deer lying in the distance, rabbits jumping around her feet, and all of it happening peacefully. The animals saw her, but didn't care she was there. Mara looked to her side to see a sharp tooth creature with black strips, whiskers, and a long tall. The tiger gently rubbed against Mara's hip. To her surprise, she was not scared.

She looked into the distance to see a mama panther and her babies playing with someone (or something). She got closer to find that it was a man. He had a black cloak on. His head was hairless. When he saw Mara, he got off the ground. The panthers moved back. Mara knew the being that now stood a small distance away from her. Verex walked close to her. She looked up at the 6 foot demon. He pushed his finger gently across her cheek. Then she laid her head down on his chest, and suddenly found herself back in her kitchen.

The next day went by slow. Mara found herself thanking of Verex all day. She couldn't even keep focus on the papers she was editing when she went to work at the publishing company on Virginia Island. Finally she got off. She paid the babysitter, and let her be on her way. It was five 'o clock. She went in the kitchen, and began to do the dishes.

After two hours of cleaning the whole house, and eating a small dinner, a knock was heard at the front door. Mara went to the door, and saw her friends and sister outside. She opened it and let them in.

"Hey girl," greeted Alisha.

"Are you ready," inquired Mara's sister, Ciara.

"Where are we going," asked Mara.

"The club," replied Dian

"Wait, I don't have a babysitter, and I'm not ready to go out," Mara fretted.

"Summer will babysit. I brought my daughter, so they can just stay here. Come on Mara," begged Ciara.

Summer was Mara and Ciara's sixteen year old cousin

"Okay, let me go get ready," Mara submitted.

They left at nine to go to a club called Domain. They sat at the bar. Mara looked down the bar to see Verex sitting, and drinking. Mara looked a Ciara, and then pointed toward Verex. Ciara didn't really understand who or what she was pointing at, just that she caught the message that Mara was moving seats. She also didn't worry what seat she was going to. Mara passed Verex, and as she did she grabbed his hand. She walked him out of the club. They went behind the building. As soon as they got back there, Mara's lips attacked Verex's. Verex wrapped his arms around Mara, and they teleported of the spot. Verex teleported them both to a suit in which they over took an intimate night.

Destiny's plan was almost complete. On July 21, 2009, Jeremiah Blair Hews was born. The council found out what had happened, and arrested Destiny, and Aphrodite. They killed Destiny quickly, but waited to bring Verex to trial to kill Aphrodite. When Verex walked into the court, he saw that Aphrodite was beat, and bloody. One of the council members gave the signal, and a guard used a magical blade to cut Aphrodite's throat. As soon as it happened, Verex fell to his knees. A tear fell from his eye like acid, it burned. Then he got up and composed himself.

"Either kill the boy, or die yourself," said one of the council members.

Verex decided to do as the council requested, and set out to kill the boy. He formed groups of demons to attack Mara over that next week. Everyday, Verex sent his strongest warriors after the boy, but Mara destroyed them all. Finally, after seeing that sending demons after her and the baby was not working, he decided to kill the boy himself.

CHAPTER ONE

RUNNING

It was midnight, the perfect time for a woman to take her baby for a stroll in the park. Yeah right, what am I talking about? Babies should go to bed early, and who would want to walk the park late at night?

Well, this woman had perfect reasons for walking the park so late at night. This woman had been through the worst of enemies the week before. Enemies you would think me crazy, deluded, for even saying where real. Demons, actual, real live demons where after this woman, or shall I say her baby.

Now don't get me wrong. This woman can handle herself to the best of them, but so many of these blood thirsty monsters had attacked her and her one year old baby that week, and that week was enough to drive a women mad!

Anyways, it was dark night, the scariest part of time. The truth is that it was the safest time to be out. See, demons lived on other plains. On these plains that demons called there own, it is a dark abyss. Only in the light of day could the demons see you. If it is dark on a human plain then it is too hard to see humans. That is aside from the demons that dwelled on mortal plains. The woman knew this. The reason she was so wise about such things was because...she was a witch.

Mara had come from a long line of witches and wizards. Her mother and father taught her about all that was magical. Her mother, and high witch of the Hews cult, told her about the rules, history, and all the magical beings. Her father told her about magical tricks, sweet tasting potions, and everything that was magical fun, but now, the greatest fun, and also love in her life would be what signed her death note. Mara was but a guard to what those demons where really after. The demons, like I said, where after her son. They were after what they called an abomination.

As Mara walked along the sidewalk under the large canopy of trees, she smiled and thought to herself, "finally, peace."

She raised her head to smell the cherry trees and felt the delightful warm air that could send chills down your body.

"Now isn't this nice Jere," smiled Mara to her son that was giddy with grins. The baby boy looked up to his mother and smiled with a giggle.

Suddenly, a deep, dark voice entered Mara's worked mind.

"He must die," said the voice.

Mara shuttered and began to stubble back as the cold voice crawled through her mind like a small spider. Mara opened her brown eyes and began to look around. The voice racked her decrepit mind again.

"Go away," she shouted.

"I can't," said the voice.

Mara heard foot steps come from the sidewalk in the distance. She prepared herself for her attacker. The steps grew louder and faster. Mara tried to see what demon the underworld had sent now. Anger attacked Mara before her real opponent had the chance. Why could they not just leave her be? What demon could not just stay in the underworld: vampires, demedarchs, or stealers?

A figure began to show in the distance. Then as it got closer Mara began to see a red jogging suit on pale white skin. It wasn't a demon. It was a man. Mara took a breath of relief and smiled at the man as he approached. He got to her and began to jog in place.

"Hello, I see you prefer the peace of the night too," said the man.

"Yeah," said Mara

"Well is it good for the baby?" said the man looking down at the baby, Jeremiah.

"Oh, he had a long nap. We don't get a lot of time to spend together," said Mara, "I just thought to spend a little time out here with him."

"Oh, okay, well be careful," said the man as he began his run again.

The words, "be careful", brought back the thought that even though the man was not a demon, somebody was talking to her. Mara took another look around, and began to walk again.

"Death will come to the boy," said the chilling voice again.

"Get out of my head," said Mara as if entering someone's mind was an everyday thing.

"Mara, it's time to end this," said the voice, but the voice had grown a new location.

Mara turned to see a tall dark skinned man standing half a foot taller than her.

"Why, how can you plot to kill your own son?" said Mara.

Without an answer, the demon pulled his left hand to his right shoulder, and swung it to Mara's face. Mara was thrown into the bushes on the left side of the sidewalk. The demon raised his hands to the stroller. Mara got to her knees and shot her hands to the front of her. A golden stripe shot through the air. The stripe was still connected to her hands as it hit the demon. The demon flew into an oak tree. Mara got to her feet and rushed to the stroller. She grabbed the baby and began to run. She turned off the sidewalk, and went into the woods.

Finally she got to the playground that lay in front of the parking lot. Mara got to her car. She put the baby in his car seat, and got herself into her seat. She started the car up, put it in reverse. Then multiple fire balls shot out of the woods. They soared through the jungle gym and past the sidewalk. Then they went into the sky, and rained back down. One hit the parking space that Mara's car was in. Mara began to drive out of the parking lot. The last two fire balls ran into a pole and street.

The car was pulling up to the club Domain when a fire ball rolled into the front of the car. The back of the car rose up, and then fell back to the ground violently. Mara was jolted forward and backwards into her seat. When she stopped herself, she composed herself enough to looked up, and see that her engine was destroyed. Mara got out, and held her hand to the front of her car. Gold electricity shot to the wreckage.

After a few seconds of casting the spell, Mara realized that her spell wasn't mending the engine. She ran to the back of her car, and got Jeremiah out of his car seat. Mara ran to the club doors. The parking lot was empty. She grabbed the handle with her free hand, and found that it was locked, and also no one was there. She waved her hand over the handle and a click was heard. Mara opened the doors, and rushed in. She hurried to a room in the back. Mara opened the door. She took off her jacket, and laid it on the floor. Then Mara placed her baby onto the jacket. The witch held her fist above the baby. When she opened it, a golden ball of light formed. The baby fell to sleep under the light. Then Mara went outside the room. She waved her hand over the door, and a golden force field appeared over it.

Then Mara walked to the main part of the club. Suddenly she turned to see that the demon was walking through the wall. When all of its body made it through, he raised his hand, and fire shot out. Mara pulled her hand up, and a shield formed. The shield was too weak and Mara was thrown over the bar. She stood up, and shot her hand to the front of her, and golden blasts of energy shot out to the demon. The demon flew into the wall behind him. Mara jumped over the counter. The demon stood up, and began to walk over to her. Mara waved her hand to the demon, and then to the door of the club. The demon flew through the door.

Then Mara threw her hands up to the doors. The doors shut and a shield formed over it. The demon Verex got up off the concrete. He held his hands up to the door then threw his hands back to the back of himself. The doors flew off their hinges. Then he punched the shield, and made it crack.

Mara ran to the room where the baby was. She waved her hand, and the shield disappeared. She went inside the room of boxes, microphones, glasses from the bar, and the baby boy that lay on the jacket in the middle of the floor. Mara picked up the baby boy, and wrapped him in the jacket.

"What was that spell?" thought Mara to herself. "Oh, uh, cast my spell, hear my rhyme, send my son, forward in time," said Mara.

A baby blue portal formed two feet in front of Mara. With tears Mara kissed the baby gently on the head. She let him float into the portal as the door to the room was broken down. The baby began to disappear into the distance of the portal, leaving his mother to her deadly fait.

Chapter Two

YEAR 2028

The portal opened up in front of an orphanage. The baby floated out, and landed gently on the porch. He did not cry that night. He was just laying there in thought. So much entered this boys mind then any other baby his age. It was like he knew his mother had just died. That he knew that she had just died at the hand of his father. The question of why his father would try to kill him and succeed killing his mother bewildered him.

The baby began to fall to sleep with the questions running wild through his mind. A few hours later he was awoken to the sound of an old woman's voice

"Oh dear, you poor thing," said the old woman as she picked the baby up, and went back into the orphanage. The door that closed read:

Ms. Loveless'
Orphanage for Young One

She went into the kitchen, and opened the cabinet door. She pulled out a wire and stuck one end on the baby's forehead. Then put the other end into a remote like object. The screen read 102 degrees Fahrenheit.

"Ugh, you have a fever." said Ms. Loveless.

She took out a bottle that had purple liquid in it and put a droplet in the baby boy's mouth. Then she went down a large hallway and went into a room that could fit twelve large hallways in it. The room was filled with cribs of other babies.

Ms. Loveless put the baby boy in a nearby crib. She took the jacket off the baby boy that his mother gave to him. She felt through it and found a wallet. She opened it and read the license.

Mara Hews, thought Ms. Loveless, "that is odd the drivers license expired in 2012."

Then she looked at the pictures and saw the little boy. She pulled the picture out of its pocket, and turned it over to read the back.

Jeremiah Hews,
Born 2009

Ms. Loveless made a weird face, and put the wallet and jacket on a chair beside the crib. Then she pulled up a mini screen that was attached to the crib. The screen lit up baby blue. It gave the choices of, hot, warm, medium warm, low warm, medium cool, and cool. She picked medium warm, and then tested if what she did, worked by filling inside the crib. After filling the warmth of the crib, she went out of the room. An hour later was seven o' clock. The workers of the orphanage came in to get the other babies. Older kids looked through the door at Jeremiah. After the workers were finished they went back out of the room. Ms. Loveless came in to check on Jeremiah.

She felt his head, and said, "Good, his fever broke."

She turned to go back to the doors that lead to the large hallway.

As she got to the kids she said, "Come on let the babies sleep."

[Six years later]

"The kids here are very nice. The boys are gentle men, and girls are very nice young ladies. Now what is it that you are looking for," said Kaitlin the new replacement for Ms. Loveless.

"Well, I would like a boy around seven years old," said Veronica.

"Now isn't that something. We only have three more boys that age. I am like seven year old boys are all the rage," said Kaitlin, "This way."

They went down a hallway to a room. Three boys lined up quickly.

"This is Daniel," said Kaitlin as she pointed to the first boy. He had blonde hair, almost pale, white skin, and blue eyes.

"This is Jake," said Kaitlin as she pointed to the second boy. Jake had burnet hair, brown eyes, and tan skin.

"This is Jeremiah," said Kaitlin as she pointed to the last boy. Jeremiah had brown, curly hair, brown eyes, and caramel skin.

"Now, uh Daniel, Jake, come over here so Ms. Dwell can see you. Jeremiah you can go unpack," said Kaitlin

"Wait, why," said Veronica

Kaitlin thought for a second, and then said, "Well I know you don't want a, mixed kid do you. I mean really." Kaitlin had said this like it was perfectly normal to ask.

"In fact I do," said Veronica

"Okay let's stop joking. Pick one of these kids that won't mess up your life or throw off the balance of nature," said Kaitlin with a little more anger.

"What is wrong with you? How could you say that," started Veronica.

"You can't possibly really, truly wont him?" asked Kaitlin, trying everything to get Veronica to change her mind.

"Yes I do," Veronica said sternly.

Kaitlin decided that trying to get Veronica to change her mind wasn't working, so she finally said, "Well he is not for sell."

Though for a second, Veronica could have sworn that Kaitlin's pupils became shaped like crystals, as if Kaitlin had a bit of cat in her.

Kaitlin grabbed Jeremiah by his shoulders, and shoved him to his suit case.

"Stop!" shouted Veronica as she came up behind Kaitlin, and grabbed her shoulder.

Kaitlin turned and punched Veronica. Veronica grabbed her cheek. Kaitlin gave a loud scream and began to hold her fist.

"You're a witch," said Kaitlin.

"Look, your crazy, and I'm not leaving you here with these kids," said Veronica.

"You think that you can stop Verex from having him witch," said Kaitlin.

Without taken her gaze off Kaitlin, Veronica held her hand out to Jeremiah.

"Come on," she said with her voice almost at a whisper. Veronica stopped looking at Kaitlin.

Then she snapped her vision back and said, "I am going to make sure you're fired. These kids don't deserve someone like you.

Veronica took Jeremiah out of the room. When they got to the office, Veronica took the adoption papers. She went to the back of the car, and got Jeremiah into his seat. Then she went to the driver seat and sat down. She started the car up, and closed the door. She looked out the window to see Kaitlin in front of the door of the orphanage. Veronica turned to look at the street in front of her, and began to drive. She looked back one more time to find nothing but a cat sitting in front of the door now.

"How long did you have to live with her as your orphan mother," said Veronica.

"Who?" asked Jeremiah?

"Kaitlin," said Veronica.

"That wasn't Kaitlin," said Jeremiah.

"What? Who was it then," said Veronica.

He did not answer. He just began to look out his window.

"Okay, we don't have to talk about it right now. I think your going to like your new home," smiled Veronica.

They pulled up to a two story brown-brick house. Veronica parked in the driveway. She got out and went to the back door to help Jeremiah out. Jeremiah slowly unbuckled his seatbelt, and then, just as slowly, got out of his seat. Veronica walked him up to the white wood door. She unlocked the door, and opened it. She let Jeremiah go in ahead of her. He walked past the kitchen, and into the living room.

"Ok now down this hallway is a game room, and an office room. Dinner is fixed around six or seven. You can eat breakfast when you get up and lunch when ever you get hungry after breakfast, but I think that there is something you will like a lot more than the food schedule; your bedroom," said Veronica as she pointed to the stairs.

Jeremiah ran to the staircase, and went up them quickly. Veronica ran after him. They got to the top and found themselves in a hallway. At one end were a closed door and a bathroom. At the other was a door that was cracked. Veronica pointed to the door that was cracked. Jeremiah ran to the door and opened it. The room was filled with the colors of space. Planets, stars, meteors, and all kinds of objects, from outer space, where on the blankets of his bed, and also the wallpaper of his wall. Jeremiah ran to his bed, and jumped on it. He hugged the covers and smiled.

The next week, Veronica went up to the court to report the woman who had tried so hard to keep Jeremiah in the orphanage. The court gave the news that the woman was dead. Found in the basement of the orphanage, stabbed to death. They told her that Kaitlin had died two weeks ago. Though if Kaitlin had died two weeks ago, then who was the woman that Veronica met. She thought of the conversation that she had with Jeremiah. That wasn't Kaitlin, was what Jeremiah had said. After the next few months of investigation on the murder, they gave up. They could not find who killed the real Kaitlin, but Veronica new it was the woman she met. It was to confusing to be able to say anything because it was still confusing for her. Jeremiah wouldn't say anything on the subject, so she had to give up. She was not going to force a child to think of something that he didn't want to.

The court did give some good news, if you would call it that. Veronica was to become the new owner of the orphanage. The judge had looked over her files and needed a new owner. Veronica took that offer.

Chapter Three

BIRTHRIGHT

[Seven years later]

"Come on Colin," shouted Jeremiah to his brother.

Jeremiah had grown into a fit, young man. He had grown a whole foot. His brother Colin was a new boy who came to the orphanage. Veronica had adopted him. He had almost pale skin, dirty, blonde hair, and brown eyes. He was a half a foot smaller then Jeremiah.

"Colin!" Jeremiah shouted to his brother, "mom has already gone to work. If we miss the bus, then we won't have a ride to school."

Colin walked into the kitchen where Jeremiah was.

"Then get a drivers license," said Colin

"Hah, funny," said Jeremiah

"I know right," said Colin

Jeremiah's impatient face did not change.

"Fine, I am ready. Chill out," said Colin.

The two of them went out side to the corner where a stop sign stood just a half foot taller then Jeremiah. A large yellow bus with tented windows rolled from around the corner. They got on the bus to see kids that where falling back to sleep, finishing their homework for first period and staring out the window.

When they finally got to school, after an hour of picking up students, the doors to the school opened by its self letting Jeremiah go to his locker. A screen appeared, and lit up green. Jeremiah put his hand on the screen and the locker unlocked.

Then Jeremiah said, "open."

The locker opened, and Jeremiah got his books for first and second period. Then surprise attacked him as his locker slammed shut.

"She is back," said Troy, one of Jeremiahs friends, "Mya has come back from New York."

"Is she here now," said Jeremiah

"Yeah, I wanted to come and get you first," said Troy, "come on."

The two boys walked briskly down the hallway, and made a right to find Mya standing in front of her open locker. The screen on her locker was blue. "Mya!" shouted Troy.

Troy looked like a baby playing peak-a-boo.

"Hey boys," said Mya.

"Mya, not to say I'm not happy you're back, but what are you doing back," said Jeremiah.

"Well mom didn't like the traffic, and rush of everything, so we moved back," said Mya.

"Well I'm happy you're back. Hey, why don't you two come, and spend the night at my house. Usually my mom doesn't like for girls to spend the night, but she has known you for years now," said Jeremiah

"Yeah my mom will be okay with it. She said that she new your mom in high school," said Mya.

That night after everyone had eaten the three of them went to Jeremiah's bedroom. Jeremiah got out a chemistry set and opened the box. In containers were liquids that were all colors of the rainbow. There was also a bowl. Jeremiah set the bowl in the middle of the three of them.

"Pick a color," said Jeremiah.

The three of them picked their own choice of colored liquid. Mya picked blue, Troy picked red, and Jeremiah pick green. They all put their own colors into the bowl. The bowl began to smoke up. Fumes began to rise to their noises.

"That is disgusting," said Mya.

"Why does it smell so bad?" said Troy.

"I don't know. This has never happened before. It usually just changes colors," said Jeremiah.

Suddenly they fell to the floor. The potion had rendered them unconscious, but as they sleep Jeremiah dreamt of his mother's death:

He is gone. You can't have him.

As he fell deep into the nightmare, the smoke from the chemistry set began to glow bright. Its shine became so bright that it lit the hallway even though the door was closed. Then the smoke shot out a shard of itself. It was like a red snake slithering through the air. It went into Troy's mouth, eyes, and nose.

You shouldn't have done that.

The next shard of smoke shot from its source, but now it was a blue serpent that went through the air, and went into Mya's mouth, nose, and eyes. After the last shard of green smoke entered Jeremiah, the dream became intense, and ran throughout the night. The next morning Verex struck, and Jeremiah awoke in shock. He threw his hand forward, as if to reach for his mother, and a lamp that lay beside him flew to the bathroom door. Mya was walking out of the bathroom, when she saw the lamp coming toward her, and she put her hands up. A gust of air shot to the lamp making it fly back across the room to the bedroom door that Troy was coming out of. When he saw the lamp coming, he put his hands up. His hands turned to stone, and the lamp was shattered by his palms. Troy stared at his hands, and Mya and Jeremiah looked at the shattered lamp. Jeremiah got out of his bed; a small thought crossed his mind in wonder of how he got in his bed, and went over to Troy. Mya did the same.

"What was that," said Troy as he watched the stone that covered his hands crumble to the ground.

"I don't Know what that was, but I know Jeremiah threw a lamp at me" said Mya as she turned to Jeremiah.

"I didn't mean to," said Jeremiah

"Guys!" shouted Troy, "Am I the only one who realized what just happened."

Mya and Jeremiah looked at him.

"You know what just happened," said Mya, "That's good, because I don't."

"Well maybe it was the chemistry set," said Troy

"How could a chemistry set do all of that?" said Mya.

"Well chemicals can make strange things happened to people all the time," said Jeremiah.

"Yeah right," shouted Mya.

Then Veronica's voice was heard from down stairs, "hey guys are you up?"

"Yeah mom," said Jeremiah. "Look, we got to go to school. We can talk about this later.

They all got dressed and ready for school. When the bus made it to school and the three of them made it down the hallway to Jeremiah's locker, a boy called Troy to come here.

"Where is my money," said Buddy

"Oh man, I forgot it today. I don't even have lunch money for myself," said Troy

"Well you know what that means don't you. Time to pay in a whole different way," said Buddy

"Look man, I said I forgot so back," said Troy.

"Back off, I am going to go hungry today, and you want me to back off," said Buddy.

"If you're that hungry, you should have brought your own lunch money," said Troy

"What did you say," said Buddy as he grabbed Troy by his collar.

"You heard me," said Troy as he pushed Buddy away.

"Oh, I was waiting for that," said Buddy as he threw his fist at Troy.

Troy caught it with his left hand, pushed buddy into the lockers with his right hand. Buddy had been thrown into the lockers so hard that a dent had been formed out of his body. Buddy slide out of it and then onto the ground. Jeremiah and Mya ran over to Troy. Troy was in a bit of shock.

"Come on," said Mya.

They began to walk down the hall to Troy's locker. They didn't get to far from the fight site when the librarian, Mr. Mathews, opened the door to the library. He called to them, and told them to come into the library.

"Now listen we have your back on this," said Jeremiah to Troy.

"Yeah," smiled Mya.

When they went into the library, and made it to Mr. Mathew's desk. They realized that he looked stern.

"I saw what happened out there," said Mr. Mathews.

"So you saw that it was all Troy right," said Jeremiah.

"Jeremiah," said Mya.

"Yes I did," said Mr. Mathews.

"You did? That's good," said Mya.

Troy gave Mya a confused look. Mya looked over at Troy, but then winced away from his puzzled look.

"So, am I in real trouble," said Troy.

"What would you get in trouble for," said Mr. Mathews.

"For fighting, and using Buddy's body to make a dent in the lockers," said Troy.

"Huh, well if there was a dent in the school lockers, that would be a problem, but there is not a dent on any of the school lockers," said Mr. Mathews.

"What are you talking about," said Mya.

"Yeah, the dent filled up a whole three lockers. How could you not see that," said Jeremiah.

Mr. Mathews motioned the three to the door. They went to the door, and opened it to look out at the lockers that Troy had fought by. To their surprise the dent was gone. No where to be seen.

Mya turned and looked at Mr. Mathews with an intriguing feature imprinted on her face.

"How… what…I…What just happened," said Mya.

Mr. Mathews narrowed his eyes, and took a step forward.

"Do you believe in magic," said Mr. Mathews

"What no, well in a way, what does that have to do with…," said Mya, "Wait, are you trying to tell me that magic brought the dent out."

Mr. Mathew shook his head.

"You're a crazy librarian," said Troy, "Help!"

Troy tried to open the door, but Mr. Mathews threw his hand forward to the door. A white mist formed around his hand and then shot to the door. The door slammed itself shut. The three of them backed off the door.

"Do you believe me now," said Mr. Mathews.

After he realized that he had their attention, he motioned them to sit down, and they did.

"What if I told you that you where not just magical beings, but one of the most powerful beings," said Mr. Mathews.

"I'd say you where a crazy librarian," said Troy.

"If you don't believe me then believe Jeremiah," said Mr. Mathews.

"What is he talking about," said Mya.

Jeremiah had his head down. When he looked up, he didn't seem like he was sad, but that he was in deep thought.

"He is telling the truth," said Jeremiah.

"How do you know that," said Mya.

"My mother, my real mother, died by a demon," said Jeremiah.

"A demon," said Troy.

Mr. Mathews began to speak again, "You three are guardians," said Mr. Mathews, "Protectors of the magical world. It is your job to keep the good and bad parts of the magical world balanced. Please believe me. The magical world needs you. You have to take your places. It is your birthright."

Chapter Four

Training

The next day after school, the three guardians went to Mr. Mathews house. It was a large house. Jeremiah knocked on the door. Mr. Mathews answered it within a second. He invited them in and then to the living room.

"I am glad you came. We will start with your weapons," said Mr. Mathews.

He went to a closet by the couch and opened it. It was a walk in closet. The walls where lined with swords, knives, and other weapons.

"Wow, what happened to guns. I don't think I can rock the ancient days of war," said Troy.

"Rock," repeated Mr. Mathews

"He means he doesn't think he can fight with those kinds of weapons," said Jeremiah.

"Well that is why I am here. Now pick one," said Mr. Mathews.

Troy went in, and came out with two two-sided axes. Mya went in, and brought out a straight blade. Jeremiah was last to go in. When he came out, he had a staff.

"Good. Now that that is done we must work on your powers. Mya, your power is air and ice. We will start with air. Yesterday morning, what made you use your powers? What filling did you have," said Mr. Mathews

"I felt in shock; like I needed to be protected. Yeah it's like the air came to protect me," said Mya.

"Let's try that with this the chair. I am going to throw this chair at you. I want you to blow the chair away," said Mr. Mathews

Mr. Mathews went to the empty chair beside Jeremiah. He picked it up and asked Mya if she was ready. She shook her head, and then he through the chair at her. Mya threw her hands up in hope to conjure a large wind, but nothing happened. The chair hit Mya, and then fell straight to the floor. It didn't even hurt her or knock her back at all. Her eyes went wide for a second then went back to their original size. Then she took a deep breath, and breathed out. Mr. Mathews felt the soft breeze even though he was on the other side of the room.

"Mya when I throw it this time, you have to breathe out hard," said Mr. Mathews

Mya shook her head as Mr. Mathews came and got the chair from Mya's feet. He went back to the other side of the room. Then he threw it at Mya. Mya took in a deep breath, and then breathed out also forcing her arms out. To all of their surprise, the windows and door of the living room were open. A blast of wind shot into the room. The chair was hit, and knocked to the wall behind Mr. Mathews.

"Ah, there we go," said Mr. Mathews, "Now,"

Mr. Mathews was cut off, by Troy saying, "I did it."

They all turned to Troy. They found that Troy's hands where stone.

"How did you do it," said Jeremiah.

"I just did what Mr. Mathews said," said Troy.

"Well, that's perfect. Now I just have you to work with," said Mr. Mathews, "Mya use your power of air more. Once you get use to it then your other power of ice will come easier.

"Jeremiah, your power is the power of moving objects and subjects. You also have the power of teleportation. Let us start with the moving objects. Think about the chair that Mya and I just used. Move it," said Mr. Mathews.

Jeremiah looked at the chair that lay sideways on the floor. He concentrated hard on the lifeless object. Then he stopped, and backed off. He thought to himself. How did he use his powers before? He was frightened in his dream. He also was….a bit mad. Jeremiah looked at the chair again. He thought of everything that made him mad, and for a teenager that wasn't hard. Then as he was at his climax of anger, he shot his hand to the side, and the chair flew right across the room.

"Good, now like I said you must use these powers more and more, so your other powers will be easier to use. Now that we are off the hard part, let us talk about your witch. This power is the easiest of creatures you maintain. Next is your vampire. A vampire looks like a gargoyle. It doesn't have a tail though. You will have the ability to move at the speed of sound. You could also hepatize by touching your opponent. Mya I don't think you will like the vampire. When you turn yourself into a vampire, it will be one of the ugliest things you will ever turn into. Then you have your first demon, and second demon. Jeremiah, your first demon is the demon of gravity. Your second demon is an earth demon. Mya, your first demon is a lion demon. Your second demon is the demon of water. Troy you demon is the demon of light. Your second demon is the demon of lava. Then you have a creature almost as powerful as your guardian, your god. Jeremiah, your god is the god of earth and all its containments. Mya, your god is the god of the ocean. Troy, your god is the god of fire. If you realize, your second demon and god are similar. The magical world doesn't know why it just is," said Mr. Mathews.

For the next few weeks, the guardians would go to Mr. Mathews' house to practice their fighting, powers, and spells. A month and a half had past when Mr. Mathews came into training room.

"Time to test what you have learned," said Mr. Mathews as he laid a bag onto a table.

Troy went and looked into the bag. He found stacks, crossed, and potion bottles.

"What are we supposed to be haunting vampires or something," said Troy with a sarcastic look upon his face.

"That is exactly what we will be after," said Mr. Mathews.

"Wait, I thought we where part vampire," said Jeremiah.

"You are, but regular vampires are evil," said Mr. Mathews, "So let's go.

Chapter Five

THE GRAVEYARD

T hey went to a graveyard that had tombstones lined in rows.
"Listen to me carefully. Stick together tonight. This is your first
fight, and first time seeing a demon up close," said Mr. Mathews.

The four of them got out of the red mustang. They walked into the
graveyard. They made it to the middle and then stopped and waited.
They began to talk about school work, and teenage drama to pass the
time. Then a scream came from behind them. They got up and ran
toward the noise. When they reached the location of the scream they
found a woman on the ground. She had large bit marks all over her
body.

"Oh no," said Mr. Mathews

"What," said Mya "Is it more than just a vampire?"

"Yes, it is several vampires," said Mr. Mathew, "Get ready."

Then forms of flying objects shot out of the sky, and attacked
Mr. Mathews and the guardians' position. They where knocked back.
Jeremiah looked up from off the ground to see a vampire standing in
front of him. Jeremiah brought his leg around to trip the vampire. The
vampire jumped in the air and began to hover. Jeremiah got up and then
ran for a building. He jumped up onto the building, and then turned

with a stake in his hand. The vampire landed beside Jeremiah. He swung his hand around to the vampire. The vampire blocked. Jeremiah threw his fist forward to the vampire. The vampire blocked that and then hit Jeremiah. Jeremiah hit the roof of the building. Jeremiah kicked the vampire in the stomach. Then when the vampire bent over, Jeremiah kicked the vampire in the face. Then he jumped up and punched the vampire two times before shoving a stack into the vampire's heart. With a scream of pain, the vampire turned stone. Many vampires flew to Jeremiah. Jeremiah pulled out his staff, and hit the closest vampire, then the next.

Mya had her straight blade out already. She was surrounded by vampires. She jumped into the air and kicked one in the face, then stabbed it when she landed. She kicked back, hitting one of the vampires in the stomach. She then pulled the sword around to decapitate the vampire. Another vampire came up, and knocked the sword out of her hand. The vampire backed handed Mya. Mya turned and then kicked the vampire in the stomach. Then she backhanded the vampire. She jumped into the air, and kicked the vampire in the face so hard that its neck snapped. A vampire came up behind Mya, and grabbed her. Another vampire began to punch her. Then Mya kicked the vampire in front of her. When it bent over, she kneaded the vampire in its nose. She then threw her leg up onto its shoulder, then the other one. With both legs on the vampire in front of her, she snapped its neck. When her feet reached the ground again, she threw her head back into the vampire that was holding her. The vampire let go. Mya swung her fist around and hit the vampire. Then she pulled out her stake and stabbed the vampire in the heart, and then that vampire joined the rest of the now stone vampires Mya killed.

Troy slammed the top part of his axe into one of the vampires, and then slammed the blade part of the axe into the vampire. He then double kicked the next vampire and then slammed the axe into the vampires head. Troy turned to see a man and two women behind him.

"Get out of here. It is not safe," said Troy

"Oh believe me. I know," said the man as he almost disappeared, and then reappeared in front of Troy.

Troy brought both of his axed around to hit the man at the same time, but the man caught his arms before they made their blow. The man twisted Troy's arms making him drop the axes. Then the man kicked Troy. Troy flew back into tombstones. Troy got up and walked toward the man. The man then grew grayish skin, wings, and claws. Troy reached to his back, and pulled out a crossbow. He shot the arrow, and it pierced the vampire's heart. The vampire turned to stone.

The women, that were aside the now stone vampire, walked up, and stood beside the statue. Then Mya came up behind the one on the right, and slammed the lady vampires head into the statue of the vampire. The other vampire lady tried to hit Mya, but was shot by an arrow and turned to stone.

"There are too many!" yelled Mya.

"Where is Mr. Mathews," said Jeremiah.

"Over there," said Troy.

When the three of them looked over to Mr. Mathew they had to turn there face because Mr. Mathews location lit up as bright as the sun. When the light began to fade they looked back. They found that all the vampires where no where to be found, but dust filled the air.

Mya looked around, and then said, "I want to be able to do that."

"Maybe someday," said Mr. Mathews as he walked past her, "It is over, and you passed."

Then the sound of a crack filled the sky. The four of them looked into the sky to see mist forming together. The mist touched down on the ground and then slithered through the tomb stoned like a white serpent. As the four of them looked closer to the serpent of fog, they saw a small figure begin to form out of the mist. Finally, a gray cat emerged from the smoke. The cat had a red dot on the top of its head.

"I didn't know a cat could do that," said Troy.

"I am no cat," said the figure that sat in front of the guardians and there teacher. "I am a Dyanight, and I have brought bad news for

the guardians. My owner has taken the guardians magic book. With the blood of fifty souls, the book can be turned from a Gramora to Gracamorum."

"Who is your owner," said Mr. Mathews.

"Arkina," said the Dyanight.

Mr. Mathews's eyes grew very wide, and then he said, "Can you take us to her."

"Not now," said the Dyanight, "but I will return to take you to the book."

With that the Dyanight was gone.

They all walked back to the car. Mr. Mathews dropped the guardians off at each of their houses.

Chapter Six

THE DYANIGHT

The next day was Monday. It was March, and only a weeks away from spring break. Colin told Jeremiah that their grandparents wanted them to come to Florida for the summer. Jeremiah new he most likely would not be able to go because of the new characteristics that he has happened upon. The guardians meet up at school and spent the day talking about the Dyanight.

"You both are going to be able to make it to Mr. Mathews' house right," said Mya.

"Yeah," said Troy, and Jeremiah shook his head.

"Good. I want help figuring out what a Dyanight is," said Mya.

"Why don't you just ask Mr. Mathews," said Jeremiah.

"I want to figure it out myself," snapped Mya.

"Fine," said Jeremiah.

The three of them walked to the school library. Mr. Mathews was in the back where students where not allowed to go, but the three guardians went anyway. Then, as they made it to the back of the isle, they found themselves in a very large room. A fireplace on each side of the room, and columns guarding each side of the fire places. Above them was a walk way that went all the way around room. Mr.

Mathews was above them, looking through books of all magical sorts. They walked forward past a couch of white and gold that matched the room. They went threw two columns to large stairs. They walked up the stairs to the walk way. Mr. Mathews didn't even realize they were there, though he bumped into Troy on his way around to another shelf. Mya walked up to a book that Mr. Mathews had sat down. It had the words, magical creatures. Mya picked it up, and looked inside. The first page read about a creature called a shirik. It said that it was an element creature that was formed out of the four elements of nature. Mya quickly turned through the pages. Finally, she found what she was looking for. The page she had turned to read *Dyanight*. Mya began to read:

Dyanight
"A Dyanight is an ancient demon. These creatures where created for the most powerful of witches. They are to serve the witches in what ever way the witch sees fit. One of the most known Dyanights was Salem. He was one of the wisest of the Dyanights. He helped his owner, Lanala Ladel, save many witches in Salem.

Spell to summon a Dyanight and gain a Dyanight as a servant: by the power that be, I call you, come to me.

I wish I may, I wish I might, call forth my own Dyanight.

"Well, that was easy," finished Mya.

"If that was so easy, then way is Mr. Mathews still looking through books," said Jeremiah.

"Maybe he didn't see the page," said Mya.

"It would be surprising if he didn't," said Troy.

"Mr. Mathew. This book has the description of a Dyanight," said Mya.

"That is not what I am looking for," said Mr. Mathews still not looking up from his book.

"Then what are you looking for," said Troy.

A white swirl formed around Mr. Mathews. Then the swirl hit the floor, and Mr. Mathews was below them. He went to book shelves down there, and looked through more books.

This went on for about a month, but the month kind of went by fast. Well in its own little way.

Jeremiah walked out of his room to the living room to see Veronica sitting on the floor. She had a box with her. He got down with her.

"What is all this stuff," said Jeremiah.

"It is all I have left of my real parents," said Veronica.

Jeremiah picked up a piece of paper. It read *Birth Certificate*. Jeremiah began to read the paper.

Father: Marvin Hews	Mother: Ciara Hews
Age: 35	Age: 32
Race: White	Race: White
Baby's birth date: September 8th 2010	
Baby's name: Veronica Hews	
Weight: 8 pounds 6 ounce	
Gender: Girl	

"Hey what was my real mother's last name," said Jeremiah.

"I believe it was…Hews," said Veronica.

"Funny. Your last name on the birth certificate is Hews."

"What," said Veronica as she took the certificate away from him? As she analyzed the paper she said, "That is, crazy."

"Maybe we are really related," said Jeremiah.

"Maybe, hey why do you have your shoes on? Where do you think your going," said Veronica.

"I was planning on going to Mr. Mathews' house today. Is that okay, said Jeremiah?

Veronica thought for a minute and then got off the floor. Jeremiah did the same, for he had finally outgrown Veronica, and did not like for her to look down at him anymore.

"I guess, but this is becoming a bit…weird don't you think. I mean you going over your librarian's house everyday."

"I don't go over there everyday."

"It is still weird."

"I told you. It is a book club."

"And when did you get into books."

"What are you talking about? I have been into books sense I could tell you the definition of what a book is."

"Alright, what is a book?"

Jeremiah looked down to the floor as if the answer was sewn into the carpet.

Then he looked back at Veronica as if she was stupid for asking the question, and said, "I don't know the exact definition, but still, you should get my point. So can I go?"

Veronica turned her head and grew a – I will regret this later- expression on her face. With the look still implanted on her face, she shook her head and said yes.

Jeremiah smiled and gave her a hug. Then he went outside and got his hover-skates out of the storage room. He put them on, and then turned them on. When he stood up, he was hovering half- a- foot off the ground. He began to push himself forward. It took him about twenty minutes to get all the way to Mr. Mathew's house.

"Good you're here. Now you can get yelled at too," said Mya.

"Yelled at? By who," said Jeremiah?

"Mr. Mathews," said Troy.

"For what," said Jeremiah?

"Jeremiah, did you happen to take the Gramora? You wouldn't have taken it out of here would you?" said Mr. Mathew.

Each of his would was drenched in anger, and a hint of despair.

"What would I want with that stinky old book," said Jeremiah?

"It is not just an old," started Mr. Mathew, but was cut off by Jeremiah saying, "stinky," and then he finished saying, "book. It is a powerful spell book, which in the wrong hands, could become a Gracamorum. Do you get where I'm going with this," said Mr. Mathews.

"You think I lost the book, and that is how Arkina got it?" said Jeremiah

Mr. Mathews turned away from him to stop the argument.

Then a crack was heard in the air. The snake of fog that they all had been waiting for had finally arrived.

"Are you ready," said the Dyanight.

"Yes," said Mr. Mathews. He had said it so fast and impatiently that it was almost a yell.

"Then let us go," said the Dyanight.

Jeremiah had blinked, and when he opened his eyes, he found himself in a swamp.

"Ewe, Yuk. What are we doing in a swamp," shrieking Mya.

"The path starts here," said the Dyanight.

They began to walk toward a forest. The weeping willows that lay on each side of the dirt path began to make loud, high-pitched cries.

"These are not weeping willows. They are shrieking willows. Magical farmers would plant these around there farm. It was a short of magical scare crow. It kept bird away, and beasts that where after the farmer's hens and fields," said Troy.

"How do you know that," said Jeremiah.

"I read," said Troy

"Read. When did you start reading?" said Mya.

"You sound like my mother," said Jeremiah.

"What. Are you calling me old? I think it is just the new make-up I am wearing," said Mya franticly.

"You're not wearing make-up," said Troy.

"Shut up," said Mya.

"We are here," said the Dyanight as it kept walking, and was followed by Mr. Mathews.

The building was a type of small castle. At the front where no door, but the Dyanight and Mr. Mathew just walked through it like it was water. The guardians looked at each other, and then walked into the castle.

As they walked in they found four onyx steps in front of them. They walked up it to find themselves in a hall like forayer. They looked forward to see the Dyanight begin to run. Then it jumped, and as it was at its climax, it disappeared in a crack of light. They realized that the Dyanight had teleported over an object that was in a stand. Mr. Mathews walked up to the book, but as he touched the book, a skeletal being engulfed in green mist grabbed, his arm. It used Mr. Mathews arm to pull itself half way out of the book. Mr. Mathews held his free hand up to the skeleton and an energy blast shot out. The skeleton shattered. Another hand tried to grab for Mr. Mathews, but he quickly pulled away.

"No," said Mr. Mathews

"What?" asked Mya?

"The book is a Gracamorum," replied Mr. Mathews

"Isn't there a way to fix it," said Jeremiah?

"Yes, but it is a powerful spell," said Mr. Mathews

"Let's try it," said Troy.

Mr. Mathews, and said, "Repeat after me. Let the darkness of yang fall from the light of yin. In this time, make this book the way it's always been."

The guardians repeated, and as they did, Mr. Mathews threw a red and white, almost silver, powder on the book. The book flew open, and a giant skeleton raised half of its body out of the book.

"Repeat the spell!" commanded Mr. Mathews.

The guardians repeated the incantation. As they finished, the skeleton was raised out of the book and turned to dust.

The guardians bent over, and grabbed their knees.

"There is your stinking book," said Jeremiah, but Mr. Mathews seemed to be paying attention to another figure.

Chapter Seven

THE TILEN WITCH

Jeremiah turned to see a woman that was sitting in a chair against the wall.

"I wondered when you would notice that I was here," said Arkina. Her hair was a dark red, and she wore tight clothes with a cloak.

"Arkina, you will be killed for taking our Gramora. It is against magical law for a magical being to take another's book," declared Mr. Mathews.

"I have done worse. Wait, you really think you are going to have it back? Well, you will never, not ever take that book," protested Arkina.

"You are mistaken witch. You are outnumbered," said Mr. Mathews.

"I do not fret over a pathetic magician, and three kids who try to call themselves the new rulers of the magical world," said Arkina.

"To bad cause I would," said Mr. Mathews as he shot an energy ball at the witch.

Arkina lifted her body into the air. The energy ball flew into the wall. Then Arkina began to laugh. As she did, three objects flew from her body. When they landed on the ground, Mr. Mathews and the guardians found that the objects where clones. All of the Arkina's pulled out zai and prepared to fight.

"Run!" shouted Mr. Mathews.

The guardians ran as the clones of Arkina came after them. The original Arkina got to the ground, and then did a cartwheel. As Arkina landed the cartwheel she kicked Mr. Mathews. Mr. Mathews flew into the stand and Gramora. When he got up he held his hand out, and a sword appeared. The guardians split up to different sides. Mya ran to the left side of the Great Hall. She went into another hall that was there just for decoration, and came to a dead end.

One of the clones of Arkina was right behind Mya. The clone threw a sai at Mya. Mya threw her hand forward, and a burst of wind it the sai. She did it again, but this time at the clone. The clone threw a fire ball at Mya's wind ball. The two forces clashed, and exploded with such a force it knocked both of them to the floor. They both jumped up, and pulled there weapon to the front of there body. Mya struck from above, but The Tilen Witch blocked with her remaining sai. Then the witch kicked her leg up into the air, and kicked Mya's arm out of the way. She grabbed Mya's throat with her left hand and slammed her head into the wall. The demon witch pulled her arm, which held the remaining sai, back. She tried to stab Mya.

Mya used her left leg to hold the witches arm back. Then Mya used her leg to push the witches arm back, and then kick the witch in the head. Mya lifted her blade up into the air, and swung fiercely down at the witch. The Tilen Witch moved out of the way. Mya pulled the sword back up quickly, and swung again. The Witch turned the sai the opposite way, and blocked. She held her hand to the wall that her other sai was impressed in. The sai flew to The Witch's hand. The zai twirled in the clones hands. Mya prepared herself.

One of the zai came from the left. Mya pointed the point of the blade to the ground, and blocked. Then she pulled it around, and knocked the sai out of the clone's left hand. Mya swung her sword around one more time, and knocked the other sai out of her right hand. The witch's clone kicked Mya's sword into the air. Mya kicked the clone into the wall. Then Mya caught the sword when it came back down.

Mya tried to stab her sword into the clone, but the clone moved out of the way. The sword went into the floor, and was stuck.

Mya turned with her back facing the wall, and sword, and elbowed the clone. She turned the rest of the way around to back hand the clone. When the clone bent over from the hit Mya kneed it in the face. Then Mya got the strength to pull the sword out of the ground, and swung it around to decapitate the witch's clone. The clone turned to ash.

Mya came out of the dead end hallway to see Troy was blocked between the clone that followed him, and the wall that made the dead end hallway a dead end. Troy kicked the clone in the stomach, and then ran for the wall. He jumped up to a high part of the wall, and slammed his axe into it. The clone got below him, and reached for his leg. Troy used his feet to grab the clone's hand. He twisted it, and it snapped. The clone stumbled back with screams raging from her throat. Troy pulled his axe out of the wall, and fell to the ground.

He swung his right axe with the blade pointed to the ground, but the left axe had the side of the axe pointed at the clone. The clone ducked the first time, but when the left axe came around, it knocked the demon clone into the wall.

She got up quickly, holding her wrist. Troy tried to strike the clone down, but the clone used her unhurt left hand to stop Troy's attack. Troy tried to strike with his left axe. The clone used her hurt right hand to stop Troy's second threatening attack. With a wince, the clone kneed Troy in the stomach. Troy returned the favor with the same hit to the clone. Troy kneed the clone again, and the clone bent down. Troy kneed the clone in the face. When the clones face shot back up, Troy pulled the axes around, and cut the clones head off.

Troy walked out of the hallway to see Mya looking down the Great hallway. Troy looked down the hallway to see Jeremiah fighting the last clone. The clone knocked Jeremiah's staff out of his hands. Jeremiah held his hand to the clone. The zai flew out of the clone's hands, and it flew back against the floor. The clone jumped up and threw a fire ball at Jeremiah. Jeremiah used his power of telekinesis to reflect the fire ball back at the clone. The clone turned to ash.

Troy and Mya ran up to him, and then they all ran toward the spot that Mr. Mathews and Arkina were. When they reached the beginning of the hall, they saw Arkina hold her hands up, and whirls of fire shot out at Mr. Mathews. Mr. Mathews flew back to the ground. When Arkina saw the guardians coming she held her hand to them. A circle of fire formed around them. Suddenly the floor flew out from under them. They saw themselves falling on different sides of a wall. They hit the ground hard.

Jeremiah got up, and began to look around. He found himself in a maze. *Mya and Troy must be in a different part of the maze,* he thought to himself. Jeremiah distanced himself from the wall of the maze, and then shot a green energy ball at it. The energy ball had no effect, so Jeremiah turned, and picked a path to walk down. After walking on the path for a minute, Jeremiah found himself at a six-way. He decided to go right, and after two minutes off walking on this path, Jeremiah found himself in a courtyard.

Not far in front of Jeremiah stood a mirror like image; an evil mirror like image. He step forward, readying himself for the fight to come.

"So Arkina thinks she can try and make a clone of me, and that will be enough," said Jeremiah

"Arkina didn't create me. I work for her brother at the moment. He is the real one you have to fear. I am a Clone. Here, let me explain it in a way in which your mind can grasp. When a Guardian is born, then a Clone is born too. Okay, you still aren't getting it. Take you and me for example. When you where born, I was born too. Though you where born of a human, I was born out of the depths of the underworld itself. I am you, only evil. I have your look and powers. The only things that are different are that I'm evil, I don't have a vampire, and I have a werewolf instead of a vampire. Also my name is different. My name is Jeremian," explained Jeremian.

"Oh, well, good to know. Now, please die easily. You know if it isn't too big of a problem," said Jeremiah.

Jeremian ran at Jeremiah, and tackled him. They twisted horizontally in the air, and then hit the metal wall of the courtyard. Jeremiah got up, and took a tight grip on Jeremian's shoulders. Jeremiah threw Jeremian across the courtyard into a wall.

"You know, I'm going to kick your ahhh," started Jeremiah as Jeremian threw his hands at Jeremiah.

Jeremiah flew into the wall again. Jeremiah sat up, and pelted his hand into the air. Stone chairs flew at Jeremiah. He ran over and grabbed at Jeremian's throat, and lifted him into the air. Jeremiah punched him several times before he threw him into the wall.

Mya was on another path fighting her counterpart. Mya's clone's name was Mia. Mya threw Mia into the wall on the right. Mia threw Mya into the wall on the left. Mya pushed Mia back into the wall. Then Mya grabbed her hair, and slung her into the ground. Mia got onto her hands and knees. Mya kicked her in the stomach. Mia fell into the wall. Mya picked her up by her hair, and then threw her further down the path. Mia got up, and ran up to Mya. Mia swung, but Mya ducked. Mia fist hit the wall. Mia back handed Mya, and Mya flew into the wall. Mia grabbed Mya by her back, and slung her to the ground. She got over Mya, and began punching her in the back of the head. Mya grabbed Mia ankles, and pulled them forward. Mia fell onto her back. Mya rolled forward, and then stood up. Mia rolled backwards, and then got up. Mya and Mia ran like track stars to each other. When they hit, they extended into the air for a minute before landing back on the ground.

Troy was at a six way crossing with his clone, Trey. They had their axes out, and were swinging ferociously at each other. Trey tried to strike from both the right and left side. Troy put his axes up to each side of him, blocking Trey's attack. Troy interlocked the axes, and then pulled Trey's axes out of his hands. Troy tried to swing at Trey with both axes on both the right and left side, but Trey caught his arms. He twisted Troy's arms, making Troy's axes fall hard to the ground.

Without a seconds delay, Trey kicked the unarmed Guardian in his stomach. Troy flew back onto a path. When Trey began walking up to Troy, he hurried himself to his feet. A shade of anger layered his mind as he ran up to Trey. Troy swung his fist around, and as he did, they turned to stone. Trey ducked then copied Troy's movement. Troy ducked, and then came up with an upper cut. Trey bent over, but just for a second. When he came back up, he back handed Troy. Troy came back with his own back hand, not hesitating to grab his opponent and slammed him into the wall. Trey punched Troy in the stomach, and then shoved him into the wall behind Troy. There faces where scratched up, and bleeding from the two's stone hands. Troy slammed Trey into the wall, and then threw him back to beginning of the path.

Trey looked up at Troy, and then said "Bordave."

The dark clone disappeared in a wave of dark red dust. Mya was in a hair lock with Mia. Mia pulled down on Mya's hair, and then pulled it back. Mia yanked Mya back so hard that Mya fell to the ground. When Mya looked up, she saw Mia disappear in dark blue dust. Jeremiah and Jeremian had columns that would remind you of Rome. They swung the columns, and they shattered to pieces. When the two realized that the columns were no more, they ran after each other, and started punching each other multiple times.

The crazy thing is that they where hitting the same spot as their opponent was hitting, at the same time. Suddenly they both hit each other in the face at the same time. They both flew back, but Jeremiah looked up to see Jeremian disappear in dark green dust. Then Jeremiah felt himself being pulled back to the hole that he fell through. The pressure of the pull became so intense that Jeremiah felt like he was a space ship flying through Earth's atmosphere. He held his eyes closed until he felt the force of the pull die off. He felt his hands, and knees settle on a cold surface. He looked up to see Troy and Mya beside him.

"Mya, what happened to your hair," said Troy?

"I got into a fight with myself," said Mya.

"Yeah, I would get that checked out. Wait, is that a bald spot," joked Troy.

"It better not be or she and I are going to have to go another round," said Mya as she felt through her hair.

"Guys!" yelled Jeremiah, "Look."

The guardians ran over to Mr. Mathews and Arkina. Mr. Mathews grabbed her throat and slammed her into the wall. He pulled back his sword to strike.

"So your brother comes to help," said Arkina.

Jeremiah held his hand out to Mr. Mathews arm so that he couldn't attack.

"What did you say?" asked Jeremiah.

"Now Matt, you haven't told him. You haven't let him know that you are his big bro," said Arkina.

"Shut up witch," said Mr. Mathews.

"Well, if you haven't, than allow me. Jeremiah, let's be smart. His name is Mr. Mathew. It kind of throws itself out there. Mr. Mat-Hews. He is your brother. Well half brother. Verex isn't his father, but that disgusting excuse for a witch, Mara, is his mother," said Arkina.

"What," asked Jeremiah rhetorically as he released his power over Mr. Mathews, or power over Matt, and the sword flew into the chest of the Tilen witch.

Chapter Eight

MR. MATHEWS NAME

The witch turned into a swirl of fire, and with a final scream, the roaring flames slammed to the ground.

"Jeremiah," started Matt, but Jeremiah just shook his head.

"What is wrong with you," said Jeremiah.

Pain was imprinted on Jeremiah's face even though it was anger that was given off as a vibe through the air.

"Why wouldn't you tell me? Why wouldn't you let me know that I didn't have to be confused anymore?" shouted Jeremiah.

Matt tried to move a little closer to Jeremiah, but Jeremiah shot his eyes to him with a devastating rage. Matt was forced off his feet, and made to fall hard on the stone floor of the dead witch's castle.

"Jeremiah, stop," exclaimed Mya. "You're not sure that Arkina was even telling the truth. She wasn't telling the truth was she?"

Mya turned to Matt for an answer. Matt looked at Mya with distress, and then looked at Jeremiah the same way.

"Forget this. I'm finished with this Guardian thing," Jeremiah said angrily.

"Jeremiah, you can't," said Matt.

"You want to watch me," said Jeremiah.

"Look I know you're mad, but there is still this demon out there trying to kill us. We need your help. Please…Jeremiah I'm scared. I can't do this without you; we can't do this without you. You're more powerful then us two. If you go, then we won't be able to fight this guy," said Mya as she got a little teary eyed.

"She is right. We do need you. You can't leave," said Troy.

Jeremiah realized that Troy wasn't really telling him he can't leave, but telling his dad that left when he was younger. Jeremiah found that the two other guardians looked to him for leadership. That he was the thread of hope that really keeps Mya and Troy from falling into insanity. Mya was too scared, and Troy needed someone to keep him strong. With this new knowledge Jeremiah walked a few steps back to Mya and Troy, and gave them a huge.

"I won't leave," said Jeremiah as a tear rolled over the caramel cheek bone of his face.

In the secret room in the library, Mya got a glass of water, and put it on the table. She held her hand over the glass of water.

"What are you doing," said Troy.

"Trying to use my second Guardian power," said Mya.

"Oh yeah, I forgot about that. I just have been using my first one. I forgot what my second power was," said Troy.

"I think it was that you can turn objects to dust," said Mya.

"Yeah that was it," said Troy.

Mya smiled and went back to trying to turn the water to ice. Troy sat down beside her, and began to watch. Jeremiah was in the front of the library sorting books, and Matt was checking books behind his desk. He walked out from behind the wooden desk, and stood a little way away from Jeremiah.

"Do you want to know everything," said Matt.

Jeremiah turned around, and said, "Yeah, it would be nice to get the full story."

"Okay. My name is Matt Brandon Hews, your brother. Our mother is Mara Lana Hews. We have the same mom, but not the same dad. My dad is dead, but it is alright. Mom never loved him. He took advantage of her," said Matt.

"Mom was a witch. Why didn't she use her magic," said Jeremiah.

"Jeremiah, there are magical laws. One of them is that people of magic can not harm mortals, which was what my father was…another is that good and evil can not mix.

The council created this law, so that a dictator does not rise up. See the council is made up of the demons of the abyss and creatures of the kingdom of light. If a creature was given the powers of both good and evil then that creature would have the power to fight them. Okay, the beings of time are becoming tired of eternal life. Destiny, Death, and the gods of Olympus, all of these beings will live forever unless the council replaces or destroys them. As we have seen it, Destiny put every bit of his skill together to get himself destroyed. He has asked his faithful friend Aphrodite to make the most unlikely of beings to fall in love. A high witch of a covenant and a general of demons fell in love throwing off everything the council worked for. That high witch was mom. The general was Verex, your father. You are the dictator. The council knows that you where born, and tried to get mom to kill you. She refused, so the council turned to Verex, who honored the council more then many seeing as he is a general. They asked him to kill you. He agreed. The council went through a year of war with the gods of Olympus. After the council won, the power of Aphrodite left the heart of mom and Verex. Verex was sent into action. He sent units that lay under his control after Mara and you. Mara fought off demon after demon. When Verex found that his plan was not working. He went after her himself. Mom was a powerful witch, so she fought him off, but Verex wasn't put in a position to control armies for no reason. Mom new this, and so she saved you, and sacrificed herself," explained Matt.

"That is way too much to take in," said Jeremiah.

"Well you took in the fact that you're a Guardian. It shouldn't be too hard to take this in," said Matt.

"I had the help of mom with that," said Jeremiah. "Hey, is there a way that we can see her," said Jeremiah.

"Oh, um, I don't think that that would be such a good thing. Mom doesn't want you knowing that I'm your brother. She will be very upset with me," said Matt.

"This is not about you," said Jeremiah.

"Come on Jeremiah. Mom is a scary ghost when it comes down to it," said Matt.

"Why would she not want me to knew," said Jeremiah.

"I don't know; she wouldn't tell me. Jeremiah, don't just think of yourself with this. Mom was very straight forward with this," said Matt.

"Think of myself," snapped Jeremiah as he narrowed his eyes on Matt.

Matt was raised a foot off the ground.

"Think of myself. I have not thought of just myself in months. You know what; don't worry about what I'm thinking. Worry about how quickly I fill like snapping your neck," yelled Jeremiah.

Mya ran to the front with Troy, and said, "Jeremiah no!"

Jeremiah looked at Mya, and then shot his eyes back to Matt. Matt was thrown back across the room. Jeremiah then turned to walk out of the door.

"Good thing that no one ever reads at this school," said Troy.

Mya gave him a stern look, and then ran over to Matt, and yelled, "What did you do."

"I'm getting really tired of being the good guy, and not throwing him across the room," said Matt.

"What did you do!" exclaimed Mya.

"He asked to see mom, and I said no," said Matt.

"Why would you say no? What is wrong with letting him see his birth mother," said Mya.

"She would get really angry if she found out, he new about me," said Matt.

"Why wouldn't she want him to know," said Mya.

"I don't know," snapped Matt.

"Hey, don't yell at me," said Mya.

"I need some air," said Matt as he disappeared in a light smoke.

"Isn't he on the clock," said Mya.

"I told you. No one comes in here. People just don't read," said Troy.

The bell rang for last period, letting Jeremiah, Mya, and Troy know that there study hall class was over. Jeremiah went to his English class. Ms. Crew was his English teacher. Her bleach blond hair curled to her shoulders. The large lines of crow's feet that marked the sides of her eyes deepened when she started to talk.

"Class, we will be learning to do research papers for the next two weeks," said Ms. Crew. "You must pick a person of history to do your paper on. This paper will have all the stuff you will have to turn into me, how to do each of these tasks, and how they will be graded."

The teacher gave Jeremiah his papers, and he began to work on it.

Chapter Nine

Battle at Bades inn

Jeremiah was in his room working on his research paper. He had finished the note cards, outline, and rough draft. He was more then half the page of his final draft. He had Mya to go over it for the grammar and spelling. She had a ninety-nine average in accelerated English class. Jeremiah was working hard on his paper trying to get it done because of it being so close to the due date.

Jeremiah had missed all the magical lessons for the past two weeks. He tried to rid himself of Matt. Though the anger would not go away, and this brought the thoughts of his brother even when he tried so hard to keep him out. Matt was the only one who could answer all the questions he had. He was the only one who Jeremiah knew that was his blood. The only real family he knew of. How could Jeremiah erase this map to his lost life when he wanted it so much?

He turned the page, and slammed it back down on his desk. He was so angry at Matt, and even angrier that he could not banish this wizard from his mind. He realized that he was writing on the back of his final draft, and that if it was written on the back that the final draft would be counted wrong. This gave a final spark of anger that set Jeremiah off. He let go of his pencil, but it didn't fall. The pencil floated in the air. The pencil shattered into millions of little wooden shards. Jeremiah focused on the research paper. All the words on the back disappeared, and then with a shift of his head, another piece of paper lifted up.

"By the print of mind, let these words bind. Knowledge I know on Harriet Tubman, let the words appear all of the sudden," chanted Jeremiah, and words filled out Jeremiah's research paper.

The next day Jeremiah got his accelerated English book, and went to class. He sat down at the very back. Mya was sitting in the row on the left of him three seats up.

"Alright everybody, get all of your research supplies," said the teacher.

Jeremiah got all his stuff out of his binder. He organized all of it on his desk. Mya looked back to see if he had all his stuff. When Jeremiah picked his final draft up to place it to where it needed to go, Mya saw the green shimmer in the words.

"Jeremiah, what did you do?" asked Mya with a shocked look on her face.

"What?" asked Jeremiah, shrugging his shoulders, and not really looking for an answer?

"You used…magic," said Mya, trying to lower her voice with the last word that came out of her mouth, but the guy behind her still gave her a funny look. "Can I help you," Mya said to the boy.

"No. Just…you know," said the guy.

"No I don't know, so stop looking at me," said Mya. Then Mya got up, and went over to Jeremiah's desk, and kneeled down beside him. "What did you use magic to do your homework for?"

"Because I can," replied Jeremiah. "Why are you giving me a third degree? It is not a big thing, so chill out."

"Not a big thing. We are not supposed to use magic for stuff like that," said Mya.

"Why, cause Matt said so?" stated Jeremiah.

"No, 'cause it is not responsible. We are the guardians, so we have a curtain why to act. Do you know what, this is not it," said Mya.

"Mya, just leave me alone," said Jeremiah.

"No. I'm not letting you turn this in," said Mya as she blew a shimmering stream of air out of her mouth at the paper. The words started to disappear.

"No!" shouted Jeremiah as he shot his sight to Mya. Mya flew back onto the ground. The words started to reappear.

"Mya I'm sorry," said Jeremiah quickly as he got up to help her. "I'm so sorry," he repeated falling back onto the ground in tears.

Mya swallowed her anger, and crawled to Jeremiah.

"Go to the counselor," said the teacher finally looking down the row, "and you can go with him. It seems that you both need it."

Mya helped Jeremiah up, and escorted him out of the room.

"I don't want to go to the counselor," said Jeremiah, and his body began to sway back and forth in a green blur. After the third sway he disappeared.

The bell rang, and kids filled the hallway. Mya found Troy, and explained to him what happened. Troy convinced Mya to go with him to Jeremiah's house.

Third and forth period went by fast. Mya and Troy got on Jeremiah's bus, and went to the back of it. The bus driver was a coach, and had to finish up with his football players before coming to the buses. Many kids filled the bus before Coach got to it. The ride to Jeremiah's house was long. The bus only went the speed of a 2016 cop racer. Finally the bus came to Jeremiah's neighborhood. Troy looked over at the direction that Jeremiah's house was.

"Mya, look!" said Troy franticly.

Mya looked out the window to see a fire in the area where Jeremiah's house was located.

"Freeze!" shouted Mya, and everyone on the bus and the bus itself froze in thin air. "Teleportation," said Mya as she grabbed Troy's hand; they both teleported off the bus.

The bus unfroze, and began to roll away. Mya and Troy ran down the street. When they reached Jeremiah's house, their faces where lit up in red. A fire engine was beside the house. People where gathered on the street.

"Mya stop it," said Troy.

Mya held her hand out to the fire. As she lifted her hand up, a blast of wind hit the flames.

"Mortal eyes be blind here, unable to see the magic that has happened near" said Troy as he shot his hand above his head and a blast of red light shot though the air.

The firemen stopped the water, turned to the crowd and said, "Listen, fires are serious, no one needs to be making false calls."

"Hurry put the fire out. It was magically done. The people can't see it anymore," said Troy as he looked around at the people who seemed to be blind to the fire and the blast of wind Mya was controlling.

Mya combined her power of air and ice to make the gust of freezing winds. The flames disappeared for the most part, and Mya went into the house.

Mya heard Jeremiah yelling upstairs

"Jeremiah, where are you," said Mya, and then a crash of wood and ash fell from the ceiling. Jeremiah was on top of it.

"Jeremiah!" yelled Mya.

He began to get up as Mya got to him.

"They took my mom," said Jeremiah.

"Veronica," said Mya.

"The only mother I have left. I can't loose her," said Jeremiah with an almost inspiring passion.

When Troy walked into the house, Jeremiah began to turn into a green blur, but this time he grabbed Mya. As she turned into a blur, Jeremiah moved his teleportation to the third Guardian. When Troy was fully blurred, they all disappeared.

They reappeared in front of an abandoned hotel. It was three stories high. There was a path to a court yard that was filled with overgrowth.

Vines, trees, and tall grass broke through the concrete of the courtyard. The three of them went into the courtyard. On the concrete that remained were the words: Bades Inn.

Then a blast of wind formed in the air. In the raging wind was Mia. The clone of Mya charged through the air, and tackled her to the ground. They began to roll over the ground. Then Trey formed out of the ground in front of Troy. Troy still looking at Mya and Mia fight, noticed that a presence was in front of him. He swung his arm around, and hit Trey. Trey flew into the wall of the hotel, with such a force that the wall shattered. Troy turned to see Jeremiah was fighting with Jeremian. Jeremiah swung his right fist around, but Jeremian bent down. Jeremiah kneed him in the face. Jeremian fell onto his back against the ground. He raised his hand to Jeremiah, and Jeremiah flew up into the air as if he had been caught onto a rocket. Jeremiah fell onto the roof of the hotel.

Mya and Mia where swinging at any weak spot they could find, but both of them where dodging the other. Then Mia grabbed Mya's hair, and swung her off her feet, and into the wall. Mya was on the ground, and then Mia pulled her up, and shoved her into the wall. Mya grabbed Mia's hair, and then kneed her in the stomach. Mya pulled her arm back, and punched Mia in the face. Mia let go of Mya's hair, and began to stumble backward. Mya punched Mia in the face with a devastating right hook, making Mia turn all the way around. Mya held her hand in the air, and Mia's hair was caught in currents of wind, and flew back into Mya's hand. Mya slung Mia into the ground by her hair.

Troy was watching Jeremiah fight his clone. He was about to jump onto the broken down red roof of the hotel to help Jeremiah, when a brick wall slammed into him. Troy flew off the ground, and landed on his side. He turned over on his back, and as he opened his eyes, he saw Trey standing above him with two two-sided axes in his hand. Troy dug his hand into the stone hard ground. Trey raised his axes into the air, and swung with a roughish force. Troy pulled his hands out of the stone floor as if it where sand. He held axes in each of his hands, and used the one in his right to block. He moved the axe out of the way, and kicked Trey in the leg. Trey fell to his knees, and into Troy's knee. Troy rolled backward, and stood up. Trey got up, and wiped the blood from his bottom lip. They bolted both pairs of axes at each other. The axes intertwined. The two tugged at the axes as if playing a game of tug-a-war. After realizing there yanking was futile, they stopped and released the iron axes. With a chiming cling of the axes hitting the concrete, the two began to fight again.

Jeremiah had pulled his staff out, and so did Jeremian. They where swinging over, under, and side to side, neither where hitting their target. Blocks where formed, and cries of battle. Finally Jeremiah tricked his opponent, and knocked Jeremian off his feet. Jeremian looked up at Jeremiah from the ground. Jeremiah pulled the staff back, and imprinted the point of it into the clone's face. Jeremian lay motionless on the ground.

Trey was clutched to the back of Troy. Troy tried to remove Trey from his back, but Trey wouldn't let go. Troy pulled his head forward, and then slung it back into Trey's face. Trey let go, and as he did Troy turned his hands to stone, and also punched him in the face. Trey was out cold.

Mia was knocked out on the ground in front of Mya. Jeremian was motionless on the top of the abandoned hotel. Trey was out cold beside Troy. The three guardians regrouped in the center of the courtyard. Suddenly the clones turned to smoke, and the center of the courtyard began to turn into a swirl of darkness. The guardians fell deep into a dark underworld. Each of them disappeared within the smoke. As they fell the air became thin, and it was hard to breath. It was like breathing in a pit of fire.

Chapter Ten

BATTLE AT CASTLE TOP

As Jeremiah opened his eyes, he saw a great black castle. The land around it was desolate. The land was black with ash, and soot. Patches of fire filled the area. He looked to his back to see Mya behind him, and Troy beside him. They looked up at him, and then looked to the castle. A blast of fire, and lightning flew passed the window on the highest floor.

"Mya, get us up there," said Jeremiah.

Mya stood up, and raised her hands as a gathering of strong wind lifted them up into the air. They flew quickly to the window that the fire and lightning passed. Jeremiah entered the diamond shaped window first, and the others followed. They found themselves standing on hard stone. They where standing in a great hall. There where columns that lay across the sides of the floor, and a bottomless pit. At the end of the great hall was a stone chair, and in front of the chair was Abovon and Matt. They where fighting viciously. Using all of there power to fight each other, Abovon raised his hands to Matt, and a blast of energy attached to Matt. Abovon waved his hands, and Matt flew down the great hall toward the guardians.

Abovon saw the three, and began throwing fireballs at them. Mya deflected a few, and then joined the other two guardians behind a column. Jeremiah bent down, and reached his arm out to Matt. His body was magically dragged over to the three.

"Veronica is on the roof of the castle," said Matt. "I will take him. You three go, and save her."

The three of them shook there heads, and after a second or two, Matt got up. He shot a bolt of fire hot lightning. This was the key to run. The guardians ran to the staircase beside the doors that lead into the great hall. They ran to the top. It had begun to rain.

"Okay, there is something wrong with this picture. It is not suppose to rain in the underworld," said Mya.

"Mya stay focused," said Jeremiah.

"Jeremiah," said a dark voice from behind the three.

Jeremiah was the first to turn. He found that Abovon had Veronica by her throat over the edge.

"Abovon, let her go…wait no," said Jeremiah.

"As you wish," said Abovon as he opened his grip on Veronica.

"Mom, no!" shouted Jeremiah as he threw his hands toward Abovon, making him fly into the wall.

Jeremiah ran to look over the edge for Veronica, but she was nowhere to be found. Then a bright orange light flew over Jeremiah. A swirl of orange lights formed Veronica's body behind Jeremiah. She looked herself up and down in wonder. Then she looked up.

"Jeremiah!" yelled Veronica franticly.

Abovon came up behind Jeremiah and grabbed him by his shoulders. Jeremiah turned, and used his arms to move Abovon's arms off his shoulders. Jeremiah right hooked Abovon, and then came back with an upper cut. Jeremiah turned and pulled his leg up, kicking Abovon in the face. Jeremiah tried to right hook again, but Abovon blocked it. Then Abovon backhanded Jeremiah. When Jeremiah bent over, Abovon kicked him in the stomach, and then hit him in the back. Jeremiah fell to the ground. Mya ran up to Abovon, but Abovon grabbed her by the throat. She was lifted off the ground. Mya swung her leg over his arm kicking the demon in the face. His hand twisted off its grip. Mya held his hand twisted. She pulled it to the side with one hand, and backhanded Abovon with the other. Then she kicked him in the stomach. He flew back into the wall. When he got up, Troy punched him with his stone fist, and then punched him in the stomach with his other fist. Abovon punched Troy. Troy flew back. Jeremiah held his hand to Abovon, and Abovon flew against the wall.

"Demon of darkness, demon of fear, demon of the damned, now the damned call you near. Feel my power hear my cry, I vanquish you by witches third eye," chanted Jeremiah.

Mya joined in, casting the spell, but Abovon broke from Jeremiah's telepathic hold, and began to walk toward Mya. Mya pulled out her straight blade, and shoved it into Abovon's stomach. The part where the blade and the skin met turned to ice. Mya kicked Abovon, and he flew back with the blade still in his stomach. Then Troy joined in to the chant. The ice turned to fire. Waves of fire ran over his body.

"Demon of darkness, demon of fear, demon of the damned, now the damned call you near. Feel my power hear my cry, I vanquish you by witches third eye," said all of them together.

After two more times of saying the spell, the flames grew to be great waves engulfing his body. His body, along with the fire rose into the air. Then the guardians eyes turned to the color of their aura. All of them raised there hand to Abovon. Abovon looked down on Jeremiah, and Abovon's eyes turned black. Jeremiah's green eyes darkened, and then with a great roar of a mighty beast, Abovon exploded. The Guardian's where thrown back across the roof of the castle.

Jeremiah was awoken by Veronica saying, "Jeremiah, are you alright. Come on wake up."

"I'm okay," said Jeremiah.

Jeremiah looked up to see Matt helping Mya and Troy.

"Is it done," said Jeremiah?

"Abovon is vanquished, yes," said Matt.

"Then let's leave," said Jeremiah as his eyes turned green again, also pulling Mya and Troy into the same state. They were teleported away from the demon world, and were put back on earth.

Chapter Eleven

THE NOTE

[A month later]

"It is weird finding my family. I mean I'm happy, but it is crazy to find out I'm a witch, my adopted son is my Guardian cousin who just saved me from a demon soldier sent by a demon general who is Jeremiah's real father," said Veronica. "It is all just so much."

"Well, are you going to tell Colin," said Mya.

"I'll have to, but at least I have some time to practice what I'm going to say. He won't be back until a week before school starts," said Veronica.

"Where did he go again?" asked Mya

"He is going to spend the summer with his grandparents. My adoptive parents," answered Veronica.

"Well, how did you hide the house being burned down?" said Mya.

"Matt got him here, before he got home. It bugs me that he used magic to make Colin fall asleep until we got back from the fight with Abatron," said Veronica.

"It is Abovon, and I'm sure it was a safe spell, and was needed to be used," said Mya.

"Yeah, I guess," said Veronica

"Do you know I wish I could go on vacation," said Mya, "Matt is going to have us training extra now that we are out of school."

"About that, do you think I should start practicing magic," said Veronica, "I mean I have to live with Matt now anyways seeing as my house was burned down by magic, and is beyond even magical repair. Though, I don't think I would want to go back there because of what happened.

Veronica and Mya walked into the kitchen with dishes from dinner. Mya put the dishes in the sink, and walked over to the counter.

"Veronica!" shouted Mya.

"What is it," said Veronica.

"It is a note from Jeremiah," said Mya.

Veronica took the note, and began to read.

I am saying goodbye to you guys. I'm sorry, but I'm going through something right now that I can't explain to you. I don't know if I'll see you again, but if I don't it might be for the better. I feel something bad is about to happen to me. Don't try and find me because I don't want to be found. Veronica, I'll miss you, but I am one of two cousins you have found. Mya and Troy, you can fight the forces of evil. The two of you are very strong and powerful. I will miss the three of you.

I love you guys,
Jeremiah

"He didn't say anything about Matt," said Mya, "He is most likely still mad about what Matt did."

"What's wrong," said Troy as he and Matt walked into the room.

Mya gave Troy the note, and both he and Matt read it. After Matt read it, sadness was imprinted on his face.

"I'm sorry man," said Troy.

"I should expect this after what I did," said Matt as he looked out the window into the pouring rain.

A few miles away, Jeremiah, drenched in rain, looked back down the road from where he had just come.

Epilogue

A look into Guardians Two
Jeremiah Returns

J eremiah comes back after running away from home, but the other two guardians find that something is not right with Jeremiah. They find that Jeremiah has been infected with a parasite. The parasite has fueled Jeremiah's anger toward Matt.

Soon the parasite grows stronger and looses interest in *killing* Matt, and focuses on becoming the greatest power in the worlds. He plans on doing this by obtaining the Flame of the gods. To this he must destroy the gods of Olympus. Therefore he puts together a demon gang to fight, joins with the Vampire Queen and her army, and unleashes the mighty Titans from Tartus. Now the guardians must battle a crew of demons, join the Greek gods for war, and vanquish the parasite so Jeremiah can fulfill his destiny to become the King of the magical world. But what of this new Guardian, what is her purpose in all of this. Is she supposed to replace Jeremiah? Will it come to that? Will the guardians have to vanquish one of their own, their leader, and their friend? If they do, then maybe it will be for the best.